COOKIE'S SUPPLY LIST
(for 1000-mile trip)

100 lbs. coffee beans
500 lbs. flour
50 lbs. salt
50 lbs. baking powder
50 lbs. lard

300 lbs. salt pork
500 lbs. dried pinto beans
50 lbs. dried garlic
10 lbs. pepper
200 lbs. dried fruit
can peaches, tomatoes
3.5 gallon coffee pots
pot racks and lids
medicine
burlap bags, rope

WYOMING TERRITORY

DAKOTA TERRITORY

NEBRASKA

UNION PACIFIC

UTAH TERRITORY

KANSAS PACIFIC R.R.

SANTA FE R.R.

COLORADO

KANSAS

MISSOURI

NEW MEXICO TERRITORY

INDIAN TERRITORY

ARKANSAS

JIM STINTON TRAIL

POTTER BACON TRAIL

GOODNIGHT - LOVING TRAIL

GREAT WESTERN TRAIL

CHISHOLM TRAIL

SEDALIA TRAIL

LOUISIANA

TEXAS

MEXICO

GULF of MEXICO

MAJOR CATTLE TRAILS
1866 - 1890

⭐ CITIES
--- TRAILS
▬▬ RAILROADS
1 INCH = 170 MILES

COME 'N GIT IT!

COOKIE AND HIS COWBOY CHUCK WAGON

BY JENNIFER COLEMAN

ILLUSTRATED BY JULIE DUPRÉ BUCKNER

To - Peggy
Sending you
Texas-sized
kissings!

Jennifer
Coleman
2021

PELICAN PUBLISHING
NEW ORLEANS 2021

The word "Pelican" and the depiction of a pelican are
trademarks of Arcadia Publishing Company Inc. and are
registered in the U.S. Patent and Trademark Office.

ISBN: 9781455626168
Ebook ISBN: 9781455626175

Printed in Korea
Published by Pelican Publishing
New Orleans, LA
www.pelicanpub.com

For my mom, Lorraine, the original tough cookie. With special thanks to Michael R. Grauer at the National Cowboy Museum for sharing his expertise.—J. C.

To Ben, Melinda, Miriam and Brian, lovers of hot, strong coffee and good books. Thank you for your help.—J. D. B.

Stars still dotted the vast night sky. The sun was hours away.

Wake up, Cookie!

Getting up around three o'clock in the morning, the cook started by grinding roasted coffee beans to make strong, black coffee that was so thick "you could float a horseshoe on it!"

Trail drivers moved cattle from their home ranch to a far-off market. A typical trail drive was: a boss; 10 to 15 cowboys (also called "hands"); a horse wrangler, who drove and herded the cow horses; and a cook, who drove the chuck wagon. The cook not only had to feed hungry cowboys three times a day in rugged conditions, he also had to wake them all up.

Today's special: Hen Fruit and Chuck Wagon Chicken.

Sometimes the trail boss might give a local farmer a newborn calf in exchange for eggs ("hen fruit"). Trading a calf for eggs may sound generous, but a new calf was too weak to keep up with the herd, so the trail boss could spare to part with it.

Cookie scrambled, fried, and boiled.
He gave a shout, "There's bacon in the pan.
There's coffee in the pot!"

COME 'N GIT IT!
GET IT WHILE IT'S
HOT!

S t r e t c h and yawn.
Cookie yelled, "Wake up, cowboys!"

The early birds sauntered to the wagon with
an offering for Cookie—found firewood.

Wood was a necessity for the daily cooking. A storage area called the possum belly was attached below the center of the chuck wagon to hold good firewood or buffalo chips. The possum belly was like a hammock and could be made from the hide of a buffalo or steer.

Cowboys gobbled down the morning grub. *A h h h!*

Cookie reminded the men to help with the mess. "Put your plate and cup into the crash pan to soak after you eat, fellers."

Cookie yelled, "Wash up, pack up!"

After the animals were hitched to the wagon, Cookie drove ahead of the herd. Sitting on some of the cowboy's bedrolls cushioned the bump, bump, bumpy ride.

"Hit the trail, Cookie!" the trail master shouted.

The chuck wagon cook would need to move ahead of the group to scout a place up the trail where the cowboys would be midday. Oxen, horses, or mules might be used to pull his wagon. When he eyed a good spot to camp, he got his fire started and readied what was needed.

Dinner was at noon.
Son-of-a-Gun Stew,
Apple Butter Grits-n-Gravy,
Cowboy Coffee, Spotted Pup
(rice with raisins).

Cows grazed and cowboys
rested a spell. Cookie yelled,
"Wash up, pack up!"

Headed further up the trail
where the herd would
be in the late afternoon.
Supper at Sundown.

Hit the trail, Cookie!

Moving ten to fifteen miles a day was considered a
good day's drive. Daily travel was decided by how
much grass and water was available.

A band of antelopes traveled the wide and rollin' plains too. Settling on a spot for night camp, Cookie set up his workstation under skies that grew heavy and grey.

BOOM! CRACK!

"Uh-oh," Cookie said. "Thunder."
Lightning flashing from a distant cloud.

Rain out yonder—and a
thunder of hooves in the
distance . . .

STAMPEDE!

A stampede is when the herd of cattle suddenly took off running. Weather, a loud sound, or even a sudden appearance of a skunk or rattlesnake could trigger a stampede, which was dangerous for cowboys on horseback. Most of the time the herd would generally run in the same direction, yet cows would also randomly split off in other directions.

Panic, crash, dash, flight!
Wild, confused, dusty plight.

Herds usually had certain animals that lead the way. These leaders were important to stop a stampede. Cowboys would catch up to the cattle in the lead and try to turn them. If the cowboys could keep turning the herd, the stampede would lose momentum and stop.

After a mighty long and frightening spell, Cookie kept the course. Tonight: Leftovers!

"There's beans in the pan. There's coffee in the pot," Cookie called.

COME 'N GIT IT! GET IT WHILE IT'S HOT!

Cowboy staples were coffee, beans, and biscuits. Pinching some sourdough from the crock stored in the pantry, he mixed in more flour and water to make a heaping helping of biscuits for the hungry men.

Tumble rumble weather rolled out, cowboys moved in. Tired, hungry, saddle sore.

"Cookie! Can you fix me up?"

COWBOY BEANS SERVES 10

2 pounds dry pinto beans
1 14.5-oz. can tomatoes
2 green chilies
2 large yellow onions
1 teaspoon salt

Wash the beans and soak overnight. After soaking, drain the beans, place in Dutch oven and cover with water. Add remaining ingredients and simmer on coals until tender.

Mend and tend. Stitch, stitch, stitch!
All in a day's work.
"There's grub in the pan. There's
coffee in the pot," Cookie hollered.

COME 'N GIT IT!
GET IT WHILE IT'S
HOT!

Cookie's vittles never tasted as
good as they did this night.

Chuck wagon cooks not only served as chef, they were
also doctor, barber, banker, and dentist! His wagon
would hold general first aid and medicinal tonics.

Dr. Lord's
LINIMENT

GIVES RELIEF
for
RHEUMATISM
SORENESS
BRUISING
SPRAINS
MUSCLE PAIN

VERNON CITY · TEXAS

Dinner and day both done.
"We're stacked to a fill, Cookie!," the men yelled.

Cattle are lowing, a cowboy sings to quiet the herd.

Calming cattle with a gentle song at night was such a good way to prevent stampedes that often a trail boss would only want to hire cowboys who were also good singers!

After washing the dishes,
filling the water barrel,
and dragging wood for tomorrow,
Cookie could finally relax his weary bones.

The chuck wagon cooks also acted as a compass. He would always place the tongue of the chuck wagon facing the North Star. When the trail master started in the morning he would look at the tongue and then knew what direction he would be moving the herd.

Preparing for the next day,
the trail master yelled,

"Set your tongue before you snore, Cookie!"

In 1866, the Civil War had ended just months before. Texas cattlemen found there was money to be made by selling their cows in the north. But moving cattle north meant men on horses had to walk ("drive the cattle"), and hardworking men traveling that far had to *eat*. Clearly, there was a need for a portable kitchen that could travel with the crew. They say necessity is the mother of invention— credit goes to Texas cattleman Charles Goodnight who, by taking an old army wagon and strengthening it with extra hard axles, invented the chuck wagon.

Cowboys used the word "chuck" to mean food, so the box was called a chuck box and the wagon became known as a chuck wagon. The wagon was specially made with a sloping box on the rear with a hinged lid that lowered to become a worktable for the cook. The box perfectly fit the width of the wagon and contained shelves and drawers for holding food and utensils. Most chuck wagons measured to be about 10 feet long and 38-40 inches wide.

The chuck wagon would also be stocked with supplies needed on a cattle drive. Besides food and cooking gear, the supplies might include tools for making repairs, sewing needles, medicine, bedrolls, and rain slickers. A large wooden water barrel carrying several days' water supply for the men would be attached to the wagon's side. Also, a waterproof canvas would cover the top and keep items in the wagon dry.

Today, the chuck wagon's image endures as a symbol of the grit and hard work from an important era. In 2005, the Texas legislature named the chuck wagon the official State Vehicle of Texas to seal its importance in Texas history.

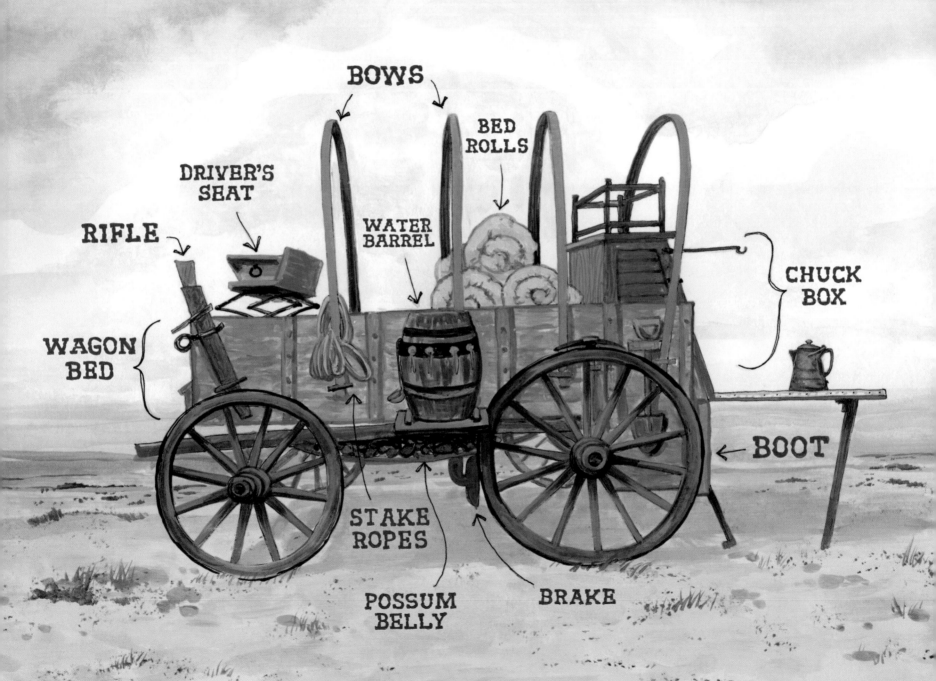

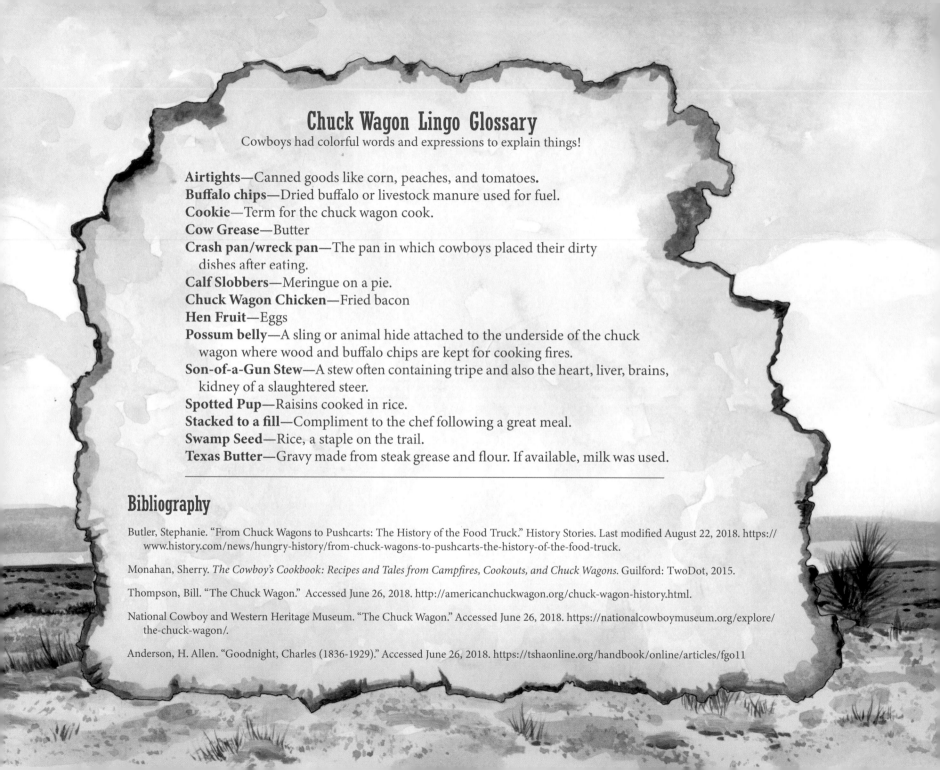

Chuck Wagon Lingo Glossary

Cowboys had colorful words and expressions to explain things!

Airtights—Canned goods like corn, peaches, and tomatoes.

Buffalo chips—Dried buffalo or livestock manure used for fuel.

Cookie—Term for the chuck wagon cook.

Cow Grease—Butter

Crash pan/wreck pan—The pan in which cowboys placed their dirty dishes after eating.

Calf Slobbers—Meringue on a pie.

Chuck Wagon Chicken—Fried bacon

Hen Fruit—Eggs

Possum belly—A sling or animal hide attached to the underside of the chuck wagon where wood and buffalo chips are kept for cooking fires.

Son-of-a-Gun Stew—A stew often containing tripe and also the heart, liver, brains, kidney of a slaughtered steer.

Spotted Pup—Raisins cooked in rice.

Stacked to a fill—Compliment to the chef following a great meal.

Swamp Seed—Rice, a staple on the trail.

Texas Butter—Gravy made from steak grease and flour. If available, milk was used.

Bibliography

Butler, Stephanie. "From Chuck Wagons to Pushcarts: The History of the Food Truck." History Stories. Last modified August 22, 2018. https://www.history.com/news/hungry-history/from-chuck-wagons-to-pushcarts-the-history-of-the-food-truck.

Monahan, Sherry. *The Cowboy's Cookbook: Recipes and Tales from Campfires, Cookouts, and Chuck Wagons.* Guilford: TwoDot, 2015.

Thompson, Bill. "The Chuck Wagon." Accessed June 26, 2018. http://americanchuckwagon.org/chuck-wagon-history.html.

National Cowboy and Western Heritage Museum. "The Chuck Wagon." Accessed June 26, 2018. https://nationalcowboymuseum.org/explore/the-chuck-wagon/.

Anderson, H. Allen. "Goodnight, Charles (1836-1929)." Accessed June 26, 2018. https://tshaonline.org/handbook/online/articles/fgo11